Samantha Alexander e with a
variety of animal including her thoroughbred
horse, Bunny, and her two kittens, Cedric and
Bramble. Her schedule is almost as busy and
exciting as her plots – she writes a number of
columns for newspapers and magazines, is a
teenage agony aunt for BBC Radio Leeds and in
her spare time she regularly competes in dressage
and showjumping.

Books by Samantha Alexander available from Macmillan

RIDING SCHOOL

HOLLYWELL STABLES

RIDING SCHOOL

6
Rachel

SAMANTHA ALEXANDER

MACMILLAN CHILDREN'S BOOKS

First published 1999 by Macmillan Children's Books
a division of Macmillan Publishers Limited
25 Eccleston Place, London SW1W 9NF
Basingstoke and Oxford
www.macmillan.co.uk

Associated companies throughout the world

ISBN 0 330 36841 9

Copyright © Samantha Alexander 1999

The right of Samantha Alexander to be identified as the
author of this work has been asserted by her in accordance
with the Copyright, Designs and Patents Act 1988.

1 3 5 7 9 8 6 4 2

A CIP catalogue record for this book is available from
the British Library.

Phototypeset by Intype London Limited
Printed and bound in Great Britain by
Mackays of Chatham plc, Kent

*Samantha Alexander and
Macmillan Children's Books would like
to thank all at Suzanne's Riding School,
especially Suzanne Marczak.*

Chapter One

"OK, you can go. I give in!" Mum threw down the tea towel. "Now, will you give me some peace?"

I was sitting on the kitchen floor, cuddling our springer spaniel, Lilly, and suddenly felt sick with elation. Was she serious? Was she really saying yes after weeks of nos, maybes, what ifs?

All my friends at Brook House Riding School were taking part in a sponsored ride over fifty kilometres of Cumbrian fells. It was a pony pilgrimage to celebrate the nine native breeds of the British Isles and was part of National Riding Week. I wanted to go more than anything in the world, but Mum was against it. It wasn't the expense. It was my asthma. She wrapped me in cotton wool even though I hadn't had an attack for ages. It had been the same when I first started riding. But now even the doctor at the hospital thought I was growing out of it.

"Rachel, did you hear me? I want to speak to your riding instructor about the accommodation. It's got to be dry and warm – no sleeping rough."

But I wasn't listening. I was already on the fells, urging Rusty on into a canter.

"Rachel?"

"Yes, Mum. Thanks, thanks a million." In three strides I was out in the hallway picking up the phone. Lilly was yapping round my heels as I punched in the familiar number. "Emma?"

I held my breath. Emma was my best friend and a member of the Six Pack, our exclusive club at the riding school. I told her everything.

"Emma, it's me, I can go!" I breathed down the phone trying to sound normal when my chest was hammering like a piston. "I'm going on the trek. Mum said I can go! Isn't it brilliant?"

"Dartmoor, Exmoor, Dales, Fell, Welsh, Highland, Shetland . . ." Emma ran out of breeds.

We were in the saloon at Brook House Riding School eating our packed lunches and talking horses. Kate, who was the eldest out of the six of us, was quizzing Emma.

"How can you go on a native pony pilgrimage ride when you can't even remember the nine native breeds? That's what it's all about!" She plucked Emma's arm teasingly. Emma screwed up her face and pinched her arm back. I whispered in Emma's ear while pretending to pull on my jodhpur boot.

"New Forest and Connemara!" she shouted out triumphantly.

"Huh," Kate snorted, "that's only because Rachel told you."

"Will you two cut it out?" Sophie interrupted, waving some papers around. "We've got better things to talk about."

Jodie and Steph walked in, making up the six members so we could start. Jodie was the best rider and wanted to be a professional showjumper when she left school. Steph had her own pony called Monty and wanted to be a horse photographer. I'd only been riding a year and was still classed as a novice. I always rode Rusty, who was the oldest pony in the riding school but the most gentle. He gave me total confidence and was really special.

"OK, let's get on with it." Sophie referred to her notes. The Six Pack were responsible for producing a Young Riders' Club news-sheet every month, which was sold at the riding school. This month the main feature was the pony trek. Sophie started to read from it. " 'The native pony pilgrimage aims to raise awareness of Britain's much loved ponies and raise lots of money. All over the country people will be taking part in organized sponsored treks, arriving at allocated horse shows where they will be performing musical rides.' "

Steph pretended to yawn. "Can't we talk about

something more interesting like where we're going to stay? Or who's carrying the saddlebags, or whether we might see wild ponies on the fells and have midnight feasts by candlelight?"

"No," Kate snapped, being bossy as usual. "And can I point out, Steph, that you have the least number of sponsors. In fact, you've only got two, your mum and dad, and you need a minimum of six to take part."

Steph howled and made a lunge for the piece of paper Kate was holding above her head. "How dare you? That's private property."

"That reminds me!" I blurted out. "I haven't got a sponsor sheet. I haven't even started yet!" Panic tore through me at the thought that I might not be able to go after all.

"Chill, Rachel." Emma grabbed my arm. "You can have some of mine. I've got loads." She pulled three sheets of paper, chock-a-block with names, out of her jeans pocket.

"That's not fair!" Steph screeched, puffing out her cheeks in a dramatic pout.

"All's fair in love and ponies," said Emma, grinning. "That'll teach you for saying I look like a sack of potatoes on Buzby."

*

"Maybe this wasn't such a good idea after all." Jodie grimaced as her mother heaved herself awkwardly onto Pirate, a heavy cob.

Emma burst out laughing as her mum's foot slipped out of the stirrup for the third time. Mrs Parker cracked up with the same infectious giggle.

Part of National Riding Week was to encourage a friend or relative to start riding and it had been Jodie's idea to invite all our mothers for a lesson with Guy. Steph was rushing round with her camera, trying hard to keep her face straight. Mum was on Ebony Jane, an ex-racehorse who was totally trustworthy and gentle. Up to now, Mum was doing the best, and I felt an unexpected swell of pride.

"It's working." Kate crossed her fingers and gave me a wink. If Mum could see that horses weren't dangerous, that riding was a fantastic sport and I wasn't at risk, then it would make my life a million times easier.

"What now?" Emma's mum gazed hopelessly at the hairy neck in front of her and looked down as if trying to find a switch on a vacuum cleaner.

"Squeeze with your legs," Mum told her as she pushed Ebony alongside, demonstrating what to do with the heels of her brown leather boots.

"Go for it, Mum!" Emma yelled as Ringo, a new

5

horse at the stable, shot off towards the field, taking her mother with him.

Kate looked narrow-lipped as she realized her own mum was still trying to get on.

Finally Guy managed to get them all in the arena and walking round in some semblance of order.

Mrs Green, Sophie's mum, was on Frank, a part-Shire gentle giant with feet like soup plates. Unfortunately she couldn't get him to move as Frank suddenly decided it was time for forty winks.

"This would be terrific in *In the Saddle*," Emma laughed, tears running down her face. "Can you imagine? *Caught on camera, mums in action.*"

Jodie's mum had dropped out of the ride altogether and was clinging on to a handful of mane instead of the reins. "She looks terrified," Kate sniggered. "I thought everyone knew to hold on to the reins."

Jodie's face instantly blackened. "Well, your mum's not doing much better," she snapped. "In fact, she can't even get on facing the right way."

The atmosphere was getting really tense. I offered everyone a fruit pastille to ease the strain.

Guy was standing in the middle of the arena, looking bewildered and out of control.

"Your mum's done this before." Steph narrowed her eyes accusingly.

"No, honestly, she hasn't," I gasped, equally shocked as my mother trotted past, hardly bumping at all.

Guy finally managed to get everyone going in the same direction and spent the next twenty minutes talking about position. As the lesson drew to a close, the Six Pack made various whooping calls and shouts of encouragement and then broke into a round of applause. Mum pulled up, fishing for a stirrup, pink in the face with excitement.

"That was brilliant," she gushed. "I can see why you enjoy it so much, Rachel. It's . . . it's exhilarating." She jumped off and removed her riding hat, her smooth brown hair not even ruffled.

Mrs Parker got stuck on Pirate and Guy had to help her off. She was bright red in the face. "Phew, that was hard work," she gasped, turning to Emma. "I don't think it's for me, love. I think I'll stick to the keep-fit on breakfast telly."

"Well, I'm going to book some more lessons," said Mum. She hadn't looked so excited for ages. "I should have been doing this yonks ago, Rachel. I never thought it could be such fun." She strode off purposefully towards the office to find Guy.

"Operation Mums accomplished," laughed Kate, giving me a high-five. "Hopefully this will be the end of all your problems, Rachel. Freedom from now on."

I touched the inhaler in my pocket and crossed my fingers. Surely now Mum had to see that horses were good for me?

A few moments later she came out of the office, beaming with pleasure, two high spots of colour on her cheeks.

"I've just been talking to Guy," she said. "He knows how I'm always worrying about your asthma. Anyway, he thinks if I have a crash course of lessons I'll be able to take one of the safer ponies on the trek. Isn't that wonderful, darling? I'll be able to come and keep an eye on you. The two of us together. Won't it be brilliant? We'll be able to ride alongside."

I could see her mouth working but the rest of my senses seemed to have switched off. It was as if I'd been turned to stone. Surely this couldn't be happening? Not Mum on the trek. Oh no. My plan. It had all backfired . . .

Chapter Two

"One, two, three . . . now!" Kate shouted, and we all turned our ponies left and wobbled across the arena.

"That was pathetic!" Jodie groaned as Emma and Buzby clashed with Kate and Archie. "We've got to keep in a straight line." Desperation started to edge into her voice.

The British Horse Society had sent us a rundown of the musical ride which everybody would be doing all over the country. It was quite simple with changes of rein and pirouettes, but relied on accuracy and timing, two things we didn't seem to have. Only two days ago, Guy had taken a video of us and played it back in his cottage and we were so bad it was embarrassing. Nobody in their right mind would want to watch us at a county show.

"You've got to count out the rhythm," Guy repeated, "and watch the rider in front. Steph, you went to sleep for most of that tape. And Emma,

you've got to hold Buzby back. You're not supposed to be on each other's heels."

"I give up." Kate pulled Archie into the middle
and dropped her reins dramatically. "What is the
point of me doing it right when Emma can't even
tell her left from her right rein?"

"Excuse me, Miss Know-it-all, but what makes
you think you're such a hotshot?" Emma turned
purple in the face and furiously tried to move
Buzby away from Archie, but to no avail. They
always stuck to each other like glue.

"What is the point of us falling out because you
bumped into each other?" Sophie was the voice of
common sense. "I'm sure everybody's trying their
best. All we can do is practise, practise, practise."

"I practise like mad at algebra but I never get
any better," Emma grumbled. Kate scowled and
levered Archie back onto the track.

"Come on, everyone," Jodie pleaded. "We won't
be able to ride for another three days. Time's
running out. Rachel, why don't you lead again?
Rusty seems quite good at it."

"What? Oh. Yes." I'd been miles away thinking
about Mum taking over at Brook House,
appearing at some time every day to have a lesson.
It must be costing a fortune and then she'd gone
out and bought new jodhpurs and boots and a hat.
A seed of resentment was growing rapidly inside

10

me. But it was silly because Mum was always trying to get me to have private lessons. She hated me working at the school for free rides but I liked it best that way. It meant I could be with my friends and get to look after the ponies, especially Rusty, and that for me was the best bit.

"Rachel, hello, is anyone in?" Jodie waved her hand up and down in front of me.

"Oh yes, sorry. I'll start at the beginning." We had to follow each other up the centre line, turn right, go down the long side, turn in and cross the arena, all changing rein and following on again. This was the easiest part and we were still mucking it up. On the day we would be joining fifty other people in the main arena and that would be much more difficult.

"Wait, wait, we can't start yet," Sophie shouted, coming up behind with Monty. "Steph's just gone to the loo."

Kate tutted, raising her eyes to heaven. "Can't she do that in her own time instead of ours?"

I turned away, smiling. Kate wasn't that bad really. She had a big heart but just liked to be in control. When I first started at the riding school she was awful but that was mainly because she was insecure. Now we all knew each other's secrets and looked after each other. One of the rules in the Six Pack was that we stuck together, no matter what.

Steph came running up from the yard, pulling her sweatshirt out of her jods. "We need to have a Six Pack meeting," she gasped as she reached Monty. "Something's come up. Sandra's just told me."

"What?" we all asked.

"I'll tell you later. But you won't like it. Not one little bit."

"How are we supposed to concentrate on the musical ride," Emma whined, "when you leave us hanging in mid-air like that?"

"Just let your mind go blank and concentrate on one thing at a time," I advised, sounding like a therapy tape.

"I've never done that in my whole life and it's a bit late to start learning now!" replied Emma.

"I'm not making it up. It's absolutely true," said Steph. She was sitting in the saloon, swinging her legs, with her arms crossed defensively. "If you don't believe me, you can ask Sandra." She tossed her bouncy blond hair.

"Of course we believe you, but Max Carrington, here, at the riding school? It'll be a nightmare." Jodie had gone white.

Max Carrington belonged to the Sutton Vale

Pony Club where all the ponies were flashy, expensive thoroughbreds and their riders spoilt and obnoxious. We'd had a run in with Max a few weeks ago when we'd been running a tack cleaning service to raise money for pony welfare. He'd been rude and horrible and Jodie had told him where to take his money. The thought of him being here permanently made me cringe with horror.

"Well, there's nothing we can do about it," Jodie said, agitated. "We'll just have to hope he doesn't ride that often."

Max was stabling his pony at Brook House because he was going on the pony trek. Nothing could be worse than that!

"It doesn't sound like his cup of tea." Emma bit her lip. "I mean, polo, horse ball, eventing, yes. But trekking?"

"His girlfriend's pushed him into it," Steph explained. "She's called Taggie and apparently he's besotted. Sandra says she's far too nice for him."

"Oh well, at least she might be a good influence," Kate said doubtfully.

Max's elder brother, Jasper, had been thrown out of the Pony Club after wrecking the annual ball. It had made front page news in the local paper. I still couldn't believe it. Max Carrington and his girlfriend stabling their ponies at Brook House until the trek since their own club wasn't going. They were going to borrow native ponies for the trek itself but needed to practise for the musical ride.

"There you are, darling." Mum walked in the door, flushed with relief. I felt a pang of guilt. I said I'd watch her have her lesson. Had I deliberately forgotten? The Six Pack fell quiet, rustling awkwardly with lunch boxes.

"Why didn't you come and watch? Guy is so good – I've nearly got rising trot already."

"Sorry." I forced myself to answer. Resentment rose inside me. This was my space. My territory. My thing.

"Come on, Pipkin, I'll take you out for lunch. Be quick and go and change."

"I don't want to," I mumbled. "And I'm not called Pipkin. That was when I was in nursery school."

Mum took a step back, her hand flying up to her mouth. I heard Emma draw in her breath. The heavy silence seemed to go on for ever. Mum looked at me searchingly but I kept my eyes down.

"It's Italian. Your favourite," she said, her voice wobbling. "I'm sure the girls won't mind."

"No, not at all, Mrs Whitehead, we don't mind a bit," said Emma.

I didn't care. I wasn't going. "No," I repeated,

14

my voice coldly polite. Even as I said it I hated myself for being so mean. But I couldn't help it.

Mum's smile collapsed. She fiddled with her handbag and then said she'd see me later. I knew I was being horrible. "Bye then, Pi— Rachel. I'll see you later. Emma, your mum is doing the rota tonight, isn't she?"

Fuss, fuss, fuss. No wonder I felt claustrophobic.

"Yes, Mrs Whitehead."

The saloon went quiet. "What's got into you?" Emma prodded me. "If I had the chance of tagliatelle in a posh restaurant, I'd be off. You wouldn't see me for dust."

"Yes, Rachel, what has got into you? Usually you don't say boo to a goose," Steph added.

"Well, maybe I'm fed up of being wet." My voice rose in exasperation. "Maybe I'm sick of being Rachel Oh-so-nice Whitehead." I slammed the lid down on my lunch box.

"But that's the way we like you," Sophie said in a quiet voice without looking up. "And we don't want you to change."

Max Carrington arrived at Brook House at two thirty with his brother Jasper and a pony and trailer.

There was instant excitement, with everyone who was waiting for the next lesson craning their necks to see who was in the trailer. There was a wild stamping of hoofs as Sandra helped to pull down the ramp. Max just watched, chewing on a piece of hay and not making a single move to help. He was blond like his brother, but thickset, bordering on plump.

A chestnut pony, about 14.2 hands, flew down the ramp, snorting and staring round, its tail cascading over its back. Sandra had a hard time leading it into the spare stable. Typically, Max did nothing.

"Yuk." Kate put a finger in her mouth pretending to be sick. "He's gross."

"Come on, let's go and stroke the pony," Jodie urged, striding forward. Kate and Sophie followed.

"What are you waiting for?" Steph dragged Emma by the arm, presuming I'd follow. But my legs had suddenly gone heavy and lifeless. A wave of shyness swept over me making my mouth dry and my stomach coil up. It had been the same all my life. As soon as there was a group of strangers, a new situation, a new face, I retreated into my shell, feeling self-conscious.

There was Emma now, going straight up to Max and starting a conversation, and there were the others, pushing in, wanting to be the first to look at the new pony. Why couldn't I be like that? Why did I have to be so shy and quiet?

16

Almost without realizing I was doing it, I started climbing up the steps to the tack room, avoiding the problem, feeling left out and isolated even though I was bringing it on myself. It was nobody else's fault. Inside the tack room it was totally peaceful and I let a long sigh puff out my cheeks, relaxing the sudden tension in my shoulders.

I picked up a copy of *In the Saddle* and started reading an article on sweet itch, but didn't take in a word. I could feel the familiar tightness starting in my chest, only it hadn't been there, not for a while. Blast! It wasn't fair. I scrabbled in my bag for my inhaler. I carried two, one for every day and another for emergencies, extra strength. It was nearly empty and I had to shake it like mad before it would work. I sucked in deep, closing my eyes as it took effect.

I didn't hear the footsteps outside, not until someone slammed back the door. My eyes flew open and I saw Max standing there, gripping a saddle and bridle and watching me with a cold fascination. His eyes lit up with an interest which made me feel nauseous. Little waves of panic started fluttering in my stomach.

"I thought I saw someone sneak off up here." His voice was heavy, thick like his body and slightly mocking. He half looked over his shoulder and let out a low whistle. "This place isn't as boring as I first thought." His eyes flicked over me maliciously. "You're a druggie, aren't you? Admit it." He lunged forward. "You're a dope-head."

Chapter Three

"No I am not!" I was outraged. I hated people's ignorance. Hated the way they prejudged. "How dare you!"

He backed up a step, his eyes registering disappointment. "Well what are you then? There's something wrong with you. You're not normal."

My breath sucked in so sharp it burnt my lungs. My hands were shaking violently. My head felt as if it was going to explode. Take deep breaths. Don't let him do this to you. Calm down. It's not worth it. I was wheezing. Max focused all his attention on me like a cat toying with a mouse.

In, out. In, out. I was getting back control. My lungs were relaxing. "You... you ignorant, rude... Haven't you ever heard of asthma?" A tear ran down my cheek and I rubbed it away angrily. "It's not the plague, you know. I have two arms, two legs and a brain that functions. I'm not weird or sick. I just happen to react to dust spores, pollen and stress. I suppose you're too insensitive to react to anything."

His jaw snapped shut and his eyes bulged with shock. "My, you're touchy, aren't you?"

"Well, wouldn't you be?" I stood up, my eyes glazed with tears. I'd had this before, right from primary school, kids pointing, giggling, holding my inhaler above my head so I couldn't reach it.

I pushed past him, heard him grunt as if I was good entertainment, and then ran for the door, tearing down the steps. I ran across the yard, sucking in gulps of air, feeling the sobs rising in my throat. Everybody was still crowded round Max's pony. Nobody noticed me climb over the field gate and stumble towards Rusty who was quietly dozing under one of the horse chestnut trees.

Rusty shifted a hind leg, then jerked his head up, stretching out behind and yawning. Rusty was a 12.2-hand Dartmoor, a strawberry roan with a cheeky, wise face. I knew if it wasn't for Rusty I wouldn't be riding. He looked after me every step of the way. Even though he'd taught hundreds of people to ride over the years, I liked to think we had a special bond. That I was one of his favourites.

"Oh Rusty, why can't I just fit in, be one of the crowd? Why do I always have to feel like such an outsider?" I buried my face in his thick wiry mane. He nuzzled my pockets. I could feel his warm breath on my hand. Max's jeering face was seared on my memory. How could people be so cruel?

"I've booked you some private lessons." Mum put the cereal onto the table next to the sugar bowl.

"What?" My head flew up.

"Well, it's about time you learnt to ride properly – none of this working for rides and messing about with your friends. Guy says you've got real ability. You could be as good as Jodie if you put your mind to it."

My mouth fell open. Was this really my mother speaking? The person who had been dead against me riding for as long as I could remember?

"But Jodie works for rides and you've just said she's really good."

"Don't answer back, Rachel, just be thankful I'm thinking of you. I thought you'd be over the moon." Mum sniffed as if she was mortally offended.

"I am," I gasped. "I really am. It's just a surprise."

A few weeks ago Mum had got a major promotion at work. It meant we could have a second car and Dad was talking about extending the house. I gazed down at my cereal bowl feeling a tingle of excitement in my stomach. I'd always wanted private lessons, just me, Rusty and the

21

riding instructor, focusing entirely on us and not having to wait our turn. I knew it was what I needed to be more confident.

But another thought slipped into my head. What would the Six Pack say? They'd call me a traitor, say I was defecting. None of them had private lessons. They'd say I was getting too big for my boots, turning into a snob.

"Rachel?" Mum looked at me sharply. "Hurry up and finish. We've got to get to the riding school. And here, I've bought you a present." She passed over a blue bag, emblazoned with the words "Haven Saddlery". Inside was a pair of cream-coloured jodhpurs in my size. They were brilliant. Just what I wanted for the trek.

"Oh Mum, they're fantastic." I leapt up, scraping back the chair, and threw my arms round her neck. "I'll go and put them on now."

It wasn't so bad after all having a new horsy mum. Not if this was the kind of present you got!

"Private lessons?" Steph screwed up her nose.

"What about the musical ride?" Emma panicked.

"Oh, I'll still be doing that. I'll still be working at the riding school," I added. "I'm just having a bit of extra tuition. It's probably a good thing.

22

It'll mean I can catch up with you lot." I laughed nervously.

"Aren't we good enough?" Steph stared at me, putting me on the spot.

"Of course." I could feel the colour sweeping up my neck into my cheeks.

"What's your mum done? Won the lottery?" Kate was sitting on the table, swinging her legs.

They were hurt. I knew it.

"Just a new job," I said. "A promotion." Kate's eyes settled on my new jodhpurs.

"Well, I think it's great." Sophie stepped forward and put an arm round my shoulder. "It's just what you need, Rachel. And take no notice of these cynics – they're just jealous because it's not them. In fact we all are." She smiled warmly and squeezed my shoulder. Jodie glared at Steph and said there was nothing in the Six Pack rules about having separate lessons.

But I still felt guilty because Sophie's dad was rich and owned half the riding school. She could have private lessons every day of the week if she wanted to. But she didn't. I was the only one breaking away to do my own thing. And I knew in my heart they were all thinking the same thought.

"Sophie, they're fantastic!" Emma went wild when she saw the special bright red jodhpurs that Sophie

23

had made for her. Sophie was really artistic and made all her own riding clothes. Emma had pestered her for a pair of bright red jods and Sophie had gone one better and stitched on pockets in the shape of a horse's head identical to Buzby's.

"Honestly, Em, I'm surprised you don't kiss that pony's hoofs." Jodie tutted. Buzby was an equine hooligan who nobody wanted to ride but Emma. No matter how many times he bucked her off or refused to move she still thought he was the best thing since sliced bread.

Emma looked at herself in the mirror, balancing on a chair to see her reflection. "There's no way I can ride Buzby bareback in from the field wearing these," she gasped, flushed with excitement.

"Well take them off then," said Kate in a deadpan voice.

"No way!" Emma looked as if she'd been asked to jump in the North Sea. I could just see Sophie's creation covered in Buzby's thick white hairs. Even in the summer he looked like a polar bear.

"Rachel can bring him in for me." She smiled, still preening in front of the mirror. "Can't you, Rachel?"

"Um, yeah, of course." I cringed at the thought of riding Buzby bareback. He was so mischievous that he liked to stop suddenly, slamming on the brakes, and doggy-shake all over in the hope of sliding you off. You could almost see him grinning with delight when his plan worked and someone was dislodged.

It was a Brook House ritual to bridle the ponies in the field and ride them bareback down to the stables. I usually loved it because you could feel the warmth of the pony's skin through your jodhpurs. Rocket, Monty and Archie were standing under the horse chestnut tree with Buzby still grazing at a furious pace in the middle of the field. Rusty was already in the stable, tacked up for the lead rein lesson. Buzby cleared a patch of grass like a lawn mower.

I prized open his jaw and tried to slip the bit in but he rolled his eyes at me and stuck his head in the air. There was so much chewed grass crammed in his mouth there was no room for the bit anyway.

Eventually I won the battle with a little help from Jodie who pulled out heaps of green slime, much to Buzby's disgust. I tucked in behind Monty and walked towards the stables.

I was all right until we were threading through the gate. Buzby suddenly swished his tail and, without any warning, threw himself into a head-to-tail shake which sent me slithering back towards his rump. All the other ponies turned to watch which just encouraged him more.

25

"Hang on." Sophie pushed Rocket forward and grabbed the reins. But it was too late. With a half buck at just the right moment, Buz sent me flying through the air. I landed on my bottom on a thistle and, to my horror, Mum was watching.

"Rachel!" She sounded hoarse. "What on earth are you doing? Have you gone completely mad?" Then she realized I might be hurt and shot forward, propping an arm under my elbow and searching my face for any sign of pain. This was the worst thing that could have happened. I was dying of humiliation.

"Mum, I'm all right."

"No you're not. That's the point. You're not all right. And what were you doing riding a strange pony? And with no saddle! I can't believe it!" She was white and shaking.

"Mum, stop fussing. I'm not hurt."

"But you could have been! Sophie, Jodie, what were you thinking of? I thought I could trust you. I thought you were responsible." Sophie opened her mouth but nothing came out. Everyone looked shell-shocked. Mum was causing such a scene. I wished I could disappear into thin air. I was so embarrassed.

"Look, I'm fine." I stood up to prove it.

Steph was holding Buzby who was trying to look as innocent as possible.

26

"Well, it's not on, Rachel. I never want to see you riding without a saddle again. Do you hear? I forbid it. I thought I'd brought you up to have more sense." Mum tutted and said she had to go and pay Guy for her lesson and she'd see me later.

I forced back the tears in my eyes and caught hold of Buzby's reins. I couldn't look my friends in the face. It was terrible. I felt about six. Awkwardly, I led Buz back to the stables where Steph wasted no time in filling Emma in on what had happened.

I slunk into the saloon and sat down heavily, wanting to burst into tears. A few minutes later the Six Pack filed in carefully. They didn't say a word but the tension crackled between us.

Eventually Kate spoke. "We can't have your mum on the trek," she blurted out. "I'm sorry, Rachel, but she'll ruin everything."

"Don't you think I know that?" I said, gesturing wildly with my hands. "I've been lying awake at night trying to think of ways of putting her off. It's a nightmare. I don't know what to do." I felt a huge relief talking about it. We'd all been avoiding the subject until now but it needed discussing.

"So how do we get rid of the old dragon?" Steph said, and Emma sniggered. Emma – my best friend. Even though I knew Mum had been embarrassing,

27

I still didn't like Steph calling her a dragon. She was only worried. It was as if my loyalties were suddenly being pulled in two directions. Sophie read my thoughts and tried to smooth things over.

"I think Mrs Whitehead is really nice. It's just that the trekkers from Brook House are all going to be young. I'm sure Mrs Whitehead is going to feel left out. It's not fair on her."

"Or us," Kate added.

"I'll talk to her," I said in a rush. "I never thought about that angle. She'll understand. I just think she's so enthusiastic about riding at the moment. I'm sure it'll wear off." I crossed my fingers behind my back, knowing what Mum was like when she got a new interest. But she had to listen. I had to make her.

"Now we've got that sorted out, let's get back to our plans," Sophie said, squeezing my shoulder. Sophie could easily be a diplomat when she grew up. Emma said it was because she was a Libran. Whatever the reason, without Sophie, I knew the Six Pack would fall apart.

"The native pony posters!" Jodie said, thrusting a huge pile of *In the Saddle* magazines on the table and a couple of pairs of scissors. "Get snipping!"

As it was National Pony Week and the riding school was busier than ever, we thought it would be a nice idea to put display boards of the different

28

native pony breeds up in the saloon. We had to cut out pictures from the magazines and snippets of interesting information, and stick them on huge polystyrene boards which Sophie's dad had brought from his company. I was doing the Dales pony.

"Wow, look at that!" Emma held up a picture of New Forest ponies galloping in a wild herd with mares and foals. We had two New Forest ponies at the riding school called Elvis and Faldo and they were going on the trek.

We flicked through tons of magazines, passing relevant pages to each other. My display board looked boring, with everything at right angles. If only I had Sophie's artistic flair. I put a picture of a black Dales pony in the middle and information in bubbles coming off it: *Dales ponies are famous for being fast trotters and can cover a kilometre in just two minutes when racing. For centuries, they were used as pit ponies, pulling weights of up to a ton. They used to carry coal over the north-eastern moors. Dales ponies were crossed with Clydesdales in the eighteenth century which is why they are so strong and muscular.*

"You haven't put in their colour and height," said Emma, leaning over my shoulder. "And it sounds like a history lesson at school."

Grumbling, I started again.

"Dad!" Sophie leapt up and ran to her dad who was standing in the doorway. He'd been away on a business trip to America for two weeks and we knew she'd missed him like crazy. He looked tired, probably from jet lag, and had dark smudges under his eyes.

"I've got something to tell all of you. Something very special and important." I noticed he was holding a letter in his right hand. Although Guy was now the stable manager, Mr Green was a silent partner in the school and helped with organizing the accounts and making major decisions. "All your work and letters have paid off," he said, smiling and struggling to stay composed.

"*In the Saddle* magazine has officially nominated Brook House for Riding School of the Year!"

Chapter Four

There were five other nominees. With the letter there were two glossy tickets, compliments of *In the Saddle*, for the awards ceremony when the winner would be announced.

Sophie read and reread the letter with everyone leaning over her shoulder.

"This is brilliant." She crushed her dad in a bear-hug. Steph put two fingers in her mouth and whistled and Emma started crying.

This is what we'd been working towards, ever since Jodie had suggested it when the riding school had been a shambles and about to close. Now it would be famous, the stable yard plastered all over the middle pages of *In the Saddle*, with Rusty, Archie, Ebony Jane, big Frank, Rocket, Buzby, Monty, Minstrel and all the other horses and ponies who were part of Brook House Riding School.

"It was Rachel who clinched it," Mr Green said. "I've just spoken to the editor and told them Guy would be appearing on the night along with Sandra."

"Rachel?" Kate ruffled my hair. "Are you sure?"

We had all filled in a form, listing the special events and activities our riding school had organized over the past year and saying in less than fifty words why our stables should win the prize. I'd kept mine really simple. In fact, I could remember it word for word: *Being at Brook House is like being at home. Everyone helps each other. We're one big happy family.*

I rubbed at my eyes which were suddenly watery with emotion. We'd done it! Brook House was up there with the best. I glanced round the immaculate stables and much loved horses and ponies. When I'd first come to Brook House, paint had been peeling off everywhere. The ponies were unused and unfit. The whole place had felt depressed. Now it was the best riding school in the area – in the country! But it didn't matter if we didn't win first prize. Just to be nominated was enough.

"I always knew Buzby was going to be famous," Emma wailed, totally overcome with emotion.

"How do you know they're going to photograph Buzby?" Steph responded. "It could be Monty." Then she remembered that Monty wasn't a riding school pony and shut up quickly.

"It'll be Rusty." I voiced my thoughts. "He's the

oldest pony at the school and he's given the most rides. It's got to be Rusty."

Everybody nodded in agreement for once. It had to be Rusty.

"Oh no, have you seen this!" Sophie was still reading the letter. "The awards ceremony is on the night of the native pony display at the Bifton show. "How can Guy lead the trek and get to London? It's impossible."

Mr Green took the letter and reached inside his jacket for his glasses. "There's only one thing for it," he said eventually. "Sandra will have to lead the trek."

Sandra had started off as full-time groom at Brook House but had been training for her teaching certificate and was now fully qualified.

"Sandra, can you come over here for a minute?" Mr Green waved her over from where she was mucking out Phantom. Guy had told her the important news earlier.

"Sandra, how do you feel about taking Guy's place on the trek? You'll be in total charge of fourteen ponies and riders."

Lots of riding schools were taking part in the same trek as us and I remembered it said on our information sheet that each party had to be led by a qualified instructor.

Sandra gaped. "What me?" she said, pointing at herself.

Everyone would be starting from the same point and riding twenty-five kilometres on the first day, staying over at various guesthouses and pubs, and putting the ponies into livery stables. Guy had spent ages organizing it. There was another twenty-five-kilometre ride on the second day and the day after that would finish with us riding into the Bifton showground at three o'clock to do our display.

"Well?" Mr Green slapped Sandra on the back. "What do you say?"

"Of course, Mr Green." But Emma and everyone else in the Six Pack noticed that Sandra wasn't happy. In fact she looked absolutely petrified.

I had my first private lesson that afternoon. To start with I was really nervous and kept goofing up. It was really intimidating having Guy's total attention on me all the time. I went bright red and lost my stirrups, then lost my voice and couldn't answer his questions.

Guy was totally understanding and called me into the middle and told me to relax. Once he'd flashed me his winning smile I felt a lot better. It was only Guy after all. For the rest of the lesson Guy put me on the lunge which was a new experience. He attached a long line to Rusty's bit and sent me round in a circle. Because he was in control I could concentrate on my position. This was something we never got to do in group lessons.

After twenty minutes Guy had me riding with no reins or stirrups, holding on to the front of the saddle. It was incredible. I'd never felt so at one with Rusty. When I took back my stirrups I was sitting much deeper and more secure in the saddle. Next time Guy said he'd have me letting go of the saddle which would improve my balance even more.

When I took Rusty back to the stable the Six Pack were busy picking up droppings in the field. Guy insisted on doing this to keep the grass from going rank and to limit the spread of worms. Everyone waved except Steph who was still sulking. The excitement over my lesson drained away and I felt bad for deserting them.

The saloon was empty. I sat down and quickly demolished a pile of sandwiches Mum had made for me, then started fiddling with my native breed poster, trying to make it look more interesting.

Max walked in and deliberately jumped back when he saw me. "Oh no, it's you again. What kind of weird concoction have you got this time?"

A heavy lump of dread settled in my stomach. I was trapped. I couldn't get away from him. I pushed my hands deep inside my pockets and tried to ignore him.

"Come on then, let's have a puff on your inhaler. Let's see what it does."

"Shut up," I said, shaking.

"Oh, so you've got a temper." Max leered close, tormenting. "So where is it then? Let's have a look." Before I could stop him he started rifling through my bag, tipping everything out.

"Stop it! Stop it!" I grabbed at the bag but he turned his back on me.

"A comb, a hair band, a diary. Ooh, that looks interesting. Oh, but here it is, the puffer."

"Maxwell."

A tall girl stood in the doorway. She had blond hair bobbed at her shoulder, which swung when she moved her head. She was about the same age as Kate and Sophie.

"Max, stop being such a pig. Leave that poor girl alone."

I blushed and felt more embarrassed than ever. Then she was walking towards me with an out-stretched hand.

"I'm Taggie," she said. "Short for Agatha. I'm Max's girlfriend although half the time I can't think why." She grinned, showing perfect white teeth. Miraculously, Max became a different person. Quiet, well-behaved, letting Taggie do the

36

talking. It was almost as if she had him on a leash. He even said sorry. When they went out I continued to stare after them in disbelief.

"What's the story?" Kate staggered in, pretending she was exhausted and gasping for a drink.

"I want a personality change," I said. "I want to be able to control creeps like that girl who's just walked out of the door."

"Mum, about the trek?"

"Yes, darling, isn't it so exciting? It's the best thing I've done in ages. I'm so pleased you got me involved."

I swallowed hard. Mum took a right turn, changing gear. "Well, I was wondering . . ." My breath started coming in short gasps. This was ridiculous. " . . . I'm worried about you not fitting in. I mean, nearly everyone going is school-aged. I don't want you to feel left out."

The silence hung between us for an eternity. I studied a road sign showing a humpback bridge. We flew over it and I felt my stomach flipping over. Mum looked astounded. "Don't be silly, darling. Why would I feel left out? We've got each other, you know, and it's a chance to do some mother-daughter bonding." She smiled warmly, and I knew she meant every word.

"Yes, silly me," I croaked, feeling sick.

37

"We'll have the best time ever, you'll see." She squeezed my hand. A lorry whizzed past. I tried not to think about what the Six Pack would say, or about their horrified faces when they found out Mum was still going. I concentrated on staring into the wing mirror and wondering how I would look with a bob like Taggie's.

"That's it. We did it! Perfect!" Kate gave Sophie a high-five and then hugged Archie's creamy golden neck, nearly falling off.

"Well, it would have been perfect if Buz hadn't decided to go to the toilet at a crucial moment," Steph moaned. Emma insisted he'd been caught short, but we all knew Buzby had done it deliberately.

All the regular riders at the school were having lessons with Guy or Sandra, practising the drill so they could take part in the musical ride. It was estimated that nearly fifty riders would be filing into the Bifton showground, on every breed of native pony, and riding in time to the national anthem. A fizz of excitement shot through me. I couldn't be on a better pony than Rusty. He concentrated so hard – I was sure he knew the routine off by heart. Sandra said we didn't need to practise again because the ponies would start to anticipate the movements.

38

"Rachel, Rachel?" Mum appeared over the gate, clutching two canvas saddlebags. We'd dismounted and I was just running up Rusty's stirrup leathers, ready to go back to the stables. I jerked upright, my mouth suddenly going dry. Emma's eyes fell on the saddlebags with envy and I cringed with embarrassment. I'd been looking at them for weeks in the window display of Haven Saddlery. They were perfect for the trek.

"Look, darling." Mum held one up in each hand. "These are perfect. Just what we need."

I felt the hot flush of colour sweep into my cheeks. They had to find out some time. It might as well be now.

Sandra paced on ahead of us, not noticing the Six Pack's startled faces. "So, Mrs Whitehead, you're going on the trek after all."

Chapter Five

"They're here, they're here!" Emma flew up the drive, screeching at the top of her voice.

The yard was buzzing with excitement as the two extra hired horseboxes manoeuvred into the drive, nose to tail. Behind was the coach which would take everyone to the meeting point seventy kilometres away, on the edge of the Cumbrian fells.

"It's really happening!" Steph grabbed hold of my hands and danced around. For years I'd drooled over adverts for horsy holidays in *In the Saddle*, and finally it was happening. A real life adventure.

Guy organized the horseboxes so that there was room to lower the ramps and load the ponies. The rest of the riders and their parents were gathered in a posse near the office, soaking up the excitement. Everywhere, eager ponies' heads pushed over doors, wanting to know what was happening. Butterflies swirled in my stomach.

Jodie was riding Phantom, a pretty grey Connemara who was a new addition to the riding school.

Her own horse, Minstrel, was sulking because he was being left at home. As an Arab he wouldn't be able to take part in the native pony display. Buzby had rubbed off his tail bandage and Archie had somehow managed to get a brown stain over his right eye which gave him the look of a pirate. Rusty watched everything calmly, his wise brown eyes taking it all in.

"I've got the wrong bib," Kate shrieked as she swivelled it round to read the letters on the back.

We were all wearing bibs like we did for netball at school, but instead of numbers we had the breed of our pony on the back and "Native Pony Pilgrimage" on the front. Kate quickly changed with Jodie so that she was wearing the one saying "Welsh".

Steph decided it was the right moment to announce she had sixteen sponsors and flaunted her list as if it were a trophy. Guy strutted around, shouting orders and lowering ramps. Sandra was taut with nerves but read out a list which told us which ponies were travelling in which box. Six ponies had been taken up the night before and stabled at a livery centre. Sophie led Rocket, a Welsh cob, straight up the ramp of the green horsebox. He was wearing a gorgeous multi-coloured rug which Sophie had made herself. A wave of fresh excitement coursed through everybody.

It was Rusty next. He went straight up the ramp next to Rocket. Mum was riding a skewbald gelding called Foxy who was really cheeky but totally safe. Sandra put him in next to Rusty.

"It's like loading up the ark," Emma quipped, jumping up and down.

"The animals went in two by two," Steph chanted.

After half an hour both horseboxes were ready to go. Guy was hopping with agitation because we were running late. Archie had decided that he wanted to go in the same lorry as Buzby so Sandra had to unload three ponies to swap them round.

"Are we finally ready?" said Guy, getting irritated with Sandra.

"You can see why it's cost the earth," Kate whispered. I knew that all my friends had cleared out their savings and used up their weekly allowance for months to pay for the trip. But it would be worth it. What could be better than riding on the fells, high up above everything?

Once the ponies had gone it was our turn. Sandra read from a register, ticking off our names. Max kept shouting out the wrong name until Taggie stood on his foot hard and dug him in the ribs with her crop. The ponies they were borrowing were going straight to the start.

"Oh blimey, I nearly forgot." Emma tore off to the tack room and returned with her bright pink crop. Buzby wouldn't even walk forward unless he could see a crop – that's why Emma had decided to buy an extra bright one.

"Now be careful." Emma's mum, Mrs Parker, put both her hands on Emma's cheeks. "Behave yourself and concentrate on what you're told."

Kate and Jodie were getting the same lecture. Sophie's dad was meeting us at the Bifton showground for the display. He still looked tired and stressed and Sophie said he might have to go back to America.

The coach was filling up. There wasn't enough room for all the luggage and the coach driver was getting annoyed. Jodie and Kate made straight for the back seat, flopping down next to the window. There was enough room for all of the Six Pack. If Mum demanded I sit with her I'd die of embarrassment.

"Sit here, Mrs Whitehead." Sandra patted the seat next to her and winked at me.

"Oh . . . um . . . all right then." Reluctantly she squeezed in and I flew down the aisle towards the back before she changed her mind. The driver started the engine in an effort to hurry everyone up. Guy watched from outside holding on to the various good luck mascots we'd given him to take to London.

The last person got on and Sandra put away her register.

We were off.

"Ten green bottles sitting on a wall . . ."

"Isn't it 'standing'?" said Kate, interrupting Sophie's solo effort.

"Ssssh . . ." Jodie whispered. Mum and Sandra kept glancing backwards anxiously. I slithered down the seat and hid behind the headrest.

Max and Taggie were in the seat in front and Max didn't know that Jodie had stuck a sticker on his back saying "Hit Me Hard". Taggie was reading *Just Seventeen* and Max was staring glumly out of the window.

Emma was sitting cross-legged because she didn't want to go to the toilet in case people thought she was weird. Kate fiddled with the air-conditioning, convinced she'd broken it.

Just as I was fighting a wave of carsickness, Sandra leapt up. Mum started making signs to get my attention but I stared out of the window pointedly. Max stood up to have a look. As we rounded the next corner, I sucked in my breath in amazement.

44

A whole car park and village green were packed full of ponies and riders. Two policemen were setting groups of riders off down the road and a vet was examining a hairy black pony with a stethoscope before it joined the queue. Everywhere there was bustle and excitement.

"Oh my goodness," said Steph very slowly and dramatically.

"Oh my shattered nerves." Emma held a hand to her chest. The whole of the coach had gone deathly quiet. "This is amazing."

I hadn't been prepared for quite so many ponies. There was every type; Highland, Fell, Dales, even Shetland, all bunched together in a group under a horse chestnut tree.

Sandra shouted from the front of the coach to get everybody's attention. "It's important we all stay together as a group and make our way to the checking-in spot which is at the far end of the car park. We'll then find the horseboxes and unload the ponies. But I can't emphasize enough" – and she deliberately looked at Emma who was writing Buzby's name in the condensation on the window – "no wandering off until we've checked in. I don't want any missing persons, and certainly not before we even set off."

There was a mad scramble as everyone jostled out of their seats, collecting their bags.

Max was livid when he saw the "Hit Me Hard" sign drop off his back but, confronted with a wall of grinning girls, he just grunted and shuffled forward.

"Look," Emma hissed, "there's TV cameras! We might get on the telly." Sure enough there was a man carrying a camera and a girl with a pony being interviewed. The pony was wearing a yellow sash printed with the name of a well-known horse feed.

"I bet she's raising a lot of money," Sophie whispered.

We were all in awe.

Ahead was a caravan with a queue of people outside. A list of times and different groups was pinned in the window. Sandra squinted and ran her finger down the list until she came to Brook House. We had an hour to wait.

"Not long. Not by the time we get the horses out, pass the vetting and get mounted with all the gear," Sandra said.

Each pony was to carry a rolled up waterproof mac clipped on to the back of the saddle and a lead rope on the front. They'd have their head collars on under their bridles. Nearly everyone was wearing a rucksack apart from Sandra, Mum and I who had saddlebags. We'd been sent a letter telling us what provisions to take. It was mainly food and water, snacks, chocolate and anything we might feel we needed. Sandra, as head of our group, had to carry a human and equine medical kit, a compass, a map and a mobile phone.

Sandra gave our details and was handed a pile of armbands and an instruction sheet. The horseboxes were parked in a field at the back of the car park adjacent to the pub. Eventually we spotted ours at the end of a long line. Max and Taggie had gone off to find the ponies they had borrowed.

"I can't believe it's actually happening." Jodie squeezed my arm as Phantom's grey head appeared at one of the windows. It was already getting warm and I tied my jumper round my waist, only for Mum to tell me it wasn't very ladylike. Everyone was partnered with their pony and told to stay in a group while Sandra tacked up Doris, a 14.2-hand Highland provided by the livery stables. Over near the village green, a brass band started up, scaring a group of Exmoor ponies half to death.

"Oh no!" Jodie had drained of colour and was staring ahead in a trance. Max was riding jauntily towards us on a jet black 14.2-hand thoroughbred, his mouth curved up in a challenging smile. Taggie was behind him on a chestnut with a silky fine mane and totally featherless legs.

Sandra froze. "What do you think you're doing?"

Max smirked like a Cheshire cat.

"Don't tell me they're native ponies," said Sandra.

Taggie looked really anxious. "Oh dear. Max said it would be all right."

"Well it's not," Jodie snapped. "What is the point of going on a native pony pilgrimage if you're not on a native pony?"

"I'll deal with this, Jodie." Sandra tried to show some authority. I knew Jodie was furious because she'd really wanted to bring Minstrel.

"I hope you realize you'll both be disqualified." Sandra already looked out of her depth. She rubbed at her temples as if she had a migraine. "This is crazy. I can't think what possessed you."

I could. Max was always out to cause trouble. He had that kind of nature. I shuddered just thinking what he was capable of. But Taggie? I thought she was nice. I couldn't believe she'd gone along with it. It must be ignorance.

People were already starting to give us funny looks. An elderly man leading two cobs started talking in a very loud voice. "It's shameful. There's always someone ready to let the side down. And all the work that's gone into this! It's criminal. Parents should keep their kids under control."

"What if we all get disqualified?" Emma voiced our worst possible fear. Sandra closed her eyes for

48

a minute and then passed Doris to one of the other riders.

"For heaven's sake, get off those thoroughbreds and try to keep a low profile." She trudged back to the caravan, looking grey with anxiety.

"You'll have to go home." Kate narrowed her eyes at Max. "Serves you right for trying to be clever."

"If you've ruined the trek for everyone," said Jodie, livid, "we'll make you pay . . ."

"Oh yeah? You and whose army?"

"You're selfish, spoilt, and irresponsible," Jodie finished.

"Yeah? Well you lot are sad and obsessed."

"It's all right," called Sandra, threading her way back. "You can still ride but not as part of the pilgrimage. You can't wear a bib or be sponsored. I must say they take a very dim view of this kind of behaviour. I'm very disappointed in you, Max. I'll be informing your parents."

Everyone from our group stared piercingly at him, making it quite clear he was now under our watchful eye. Taggie blushed crimson and said she'd never been so embarrassed in her whole life.

We were late for the vetting. There seemed to be even more ponies milling around than before. There was a whole wave of spectators lining the narrow village street and waving Union Jack flags.

"There's Newsround over there," Steph whispered, jerking her neck backwards and rolling her eyes.

"Newsround!" Emma informed the whole of Cumbria.

A friendly vet with a moustache and a stethoscope examined Rusty, listening to his heart and lungs and looking in his eyes. He asked me his age and name and said I looked after him beautifully. I felt like his real owner.

There were three different routes over the fells and different groups were being set off at fifteen minute intervals. I pulled on the armband which had "Brook House" written on in black felt-tip. Rusty waited patiently behind Archie, unaware of the big occasion. Luckily, Mum was busy with some of the other riders, organizing them into pairs, and I could pretend she wasn't really here at all. Blue sky broke through a knot of clouds and my spine shivered with anticipation.

"Five minutes to go," Emma said. Sandra was synchronizing her watch with the starter's watch. There was a white tape which marked the starting point and as soon as the whistle blew we could set off. It reminded me of the Grand National.

"Two minutes," said Emma. Rusty pricked up his ears, suddenly interested.

"Is everyone quite sure they've got everything?" Sandra shouted.

The starter called the first pair forward. "Just follow the arrows and you can't go wrong."

Sandra pushed Doris up to the white tape. Jodie was right next to her, Kate and Steph behind. Emma drew Buzby level with Rusty. Eight Brook House native ponies waited patiently behind.

Silence. Then the whistle. Within seconds we were trotting down the road, grinning at spectators, gazing at the awesome rise of the fells just ahead. We were here. It was really happening. Rusty quickened his step.

This was going to be the best riding holiday ever.

Chapter Six

"Wow!" gasped Emma. Even the ponies seemed to slow down, stunned at the vastness of the scenery. It was incredible.

For the past hour we'd been following a sheep track up the side of a fell, zigzagging around huge boulders, the horse's hoofs digging into the tight, short grass. Nobody spoke; everybody was too wrapped up in the experience. At the top, Sandra called a halt, dismounting and loosening the girths. There was a fresh breeze now, although it was a hot day. Even this high up, sheep were dotted about, staring at us curiously, clinging to impossible precipices, regardless of the sheer drop.

High up in the clear blue sky, a buzzard circled, gliding effortlessly, no doubt wondering who we were. Steph was convinced it was an eagle but everyone else in the group disagreed. Whatever it was, it seemed so free and regal. I stared upwards. Rusty pulled down, tugging at the coarse grass. The rest of the ponies did the same.

"We'll ride on to a place called High Tup Todd

and then stop for lunch," Sandra said. "We can let the ponies graze and there's a river there for them to have a drink."

It was a million miles away from school or chores at Brook House. Emma pulled out a bar of chocolate and a carton of fruit juice. Down below, movement caught everybody's eye.

"It's ponies," Kate breathed. "Look, a herd."

Sandra stepped closer, squinting into the bright light. "They're wild Fell ponies," she said, excited. "I think there are mares with foals."

Everyone drew in their breaths. It was like a dream. Sandra said that wild herds roamed the fells and that once a year they were brought down to the farms where some of the young stock were sent to sales. It kept the breed sturdy and strong so that they were able to look after themselves through the winter. Some of the Fell ponies at the Bifton show would no doubt be from this stock.

We had to get closer. We split into two halves, one group holding the ponies, while the other scrabbled down the hillside, and vice versa. It was too steep to ride down but the wild ponies seemed to graze effortlessly. Mum passed me the camera and Sandra said we had to be quiet and not get too close.

I held my breath, sliding down on my bottom. Tufts of wiry long grass made good footholds but

53

loose stones were lethal. Emma let out a yelp as one of her legs shot forwards. The wild ponies pricked up their ears and stopped eating. They seemed used to the sight of people but edged back when we moved closer.

"Look over there," Sophie whispered. Behind a black mare with a long mane and tail was a tiny brown foal. It nuzzled its mum's flanks and then peeked out at us from under her tummy. We all gasped and clicked our cameras. It was a priceless moment.

"I can't believe how good a condition they're in," said Jodie, hovering near my shoulder. "Considering they never have a groom or anything they look wonderful."

"Well that's it then," Steph said. "We can throw away our body brushes with a clear conscience.

"But they don't get sweated up with saddles and bridles," I said. "Our ponies would soon get sores if we didn't brush off the mud and dried sweat."

At that moment another foal shot out from behind its mum and gambolled across to us, incredibly brave. It got so close we could actually see its eyelashes. It snorted and held up its short tufty tail in a dramatic pose.

"Show off," Jodie murmured, but there were tears in her eyes as the foal edged closer, still daring danger. Suddenly its mum called out angrily and it loped back, chastised, as she pushed him behind her out of harm's way.

It was magical. Something we'd remember for ever. We scrabbled back up the hillside so that the second group could go and have a look. None of us had really expected to see wild ponies. It was getting better by the minute.

We were starving by the time we stopped for lunch. It had to be something to do with the fresh air and being so high up. Mum took a photograph of me and Rusty with the fells in the background. We'd spent the last two hours riding down into a valley with the ponies hunching their quarters and surefootedly picking their way through. Although we knew there were other groups of riders ahead and behind us, we didn't see anybody. Sometimes the ponies threw up their heads and neighed as if they had suddenly caught a scent on the breeze. Buzby had managed to devour a whole box of liquorice allsorts which Emma kept dragging out of her pocket and bribing him with. Now he didn't want to have his bridle taken off because he was too busy sucking liquorice off his bit.

"That pony'll have to have false teeth by the time he's ten," Sandra tutted.

Taggie led her pony across and sat down beside me.

"I feel terrible," she said, "as if everyone's thinking I'm a complete dork. I could kill Max."

We'd taken off the ponies' bridles so they could graze in their head collars. Taggie pulled up her knees and wrapped her arms round them.

"Why do you go out with him?" I asked, blurting out the question before I could stop myself.

"I don't. Not really. Max's parents are best friends with my parents. We've known each other since nursery school. He's not that bad when you get to know him."

"Mmm." I found that hard to believe.

"Honestly." Taggie grinned. "Your mum was telling me that you've not been riding very long. You're very good. I was following you earlier. You've got natural talent."

The colour started in my neck and flooded into my cheeks. If only there was a way of controlling blushing. It was so immature. "Thanks," I mumbled, swelling with pride. The Six Pack had told me I was a good rider but I'd never really believed them. Coming from Taggie it meant something. She didn't have to boost my confidence.

She got up then because her pony had tangled its lead rope round its legs. "I'll see you later," she said, waving.

Emma took her place, with Buzby hoovering up every blade of grass. She pulled the crusts off a tuna sandwich and threw them near a rock for the buzzard.

"I think it's more interested in live prey," I giggled.

"Good. Hopefully it'll come and grab Steph and carry her off to distant continents."

"What have you been fighting about now?" I groaned.

"Oh, you know, the usual. She thinks Buzby kicked Monty. But he didn't, not intentionally."

Emma, Steph, Kate and Jodie were always bickering and falling out. Sophie and I were the mediators, the peacekeepers who smoothed over the bad feeling and kept the Six Pack together. But it wasn't always easy.

"Why were you talking to her?" Emma said in a huff, jerking her neck in Taggie's direction.

"Because she's really nice," I said firmly. "I like her."

Emma pushed her bottom lip out, wrinkling her forehead. "You know what Kate says, don't you? Birds of a feather flock together. She can't be any good if she knocks around with Max."

"Well you can tell Kate that she shouldn't pre-judge people," I said. "Everybody deserves a chance."

A short distance on we crossed a bridge and then dropped down to the river. Rusty whickered eagerly and nosed Buzby's bottom as if to urge him on. It was hot now. We all had our jumpers tied round our waists much to Mum's distaste. Mum was doing incredibly well. She was stiffening up but she hardly mentioned it. She said the scenery was so breathtaking that it was a small price to pay.

Buzby slurped noisily at the water, dragging Emma closer to the edge and splashing water up all over her boots and jods.

"Watch out!" shouted Sophie as she got caught by a spray of water.

Rusty sipped gratefully at the fresh water as I loosened his girth and balanced precariously on a stone.

Max was just ahead trying to impress Taggie by standing with each foot on a different stone, and balancing with one arm. Mum and Sandra had gone back to find a plaster for a girl who'd just had her finger bitten. It was her own fault for giving her pony titbits without holding the palm of her hand out flat.

Steph crept up behind Max, hopping from one lichen-covered stone to the other. She pressed her finger to her lips. Oh God, I wish she wouldn't. I could feel my heart start to beat faster. She pushed Max in the back and he went stumbling into the water up to his knees.

58

"Look, everyone, it's the Loch Ness monster!"

Max cursed and spun round, his eyes blazing. But even though it was obvious Steph had pushed him in he looked through her straight at me. I swallowed nervously and turned away but he still carried on looking until I could feel the hairs on the back of my neck start to rise.

There was another tape, a steward and a vet when we crossed the twenty-five-kilometre line at Ricdoon. Emma stood in her stirrups and punched the air in triumph and we all did the same, even Mum. I threw my arms round Rusty's neck and thanked him for the best ride ever. It had been ace. Even better than we'd dreamed.

"The stables are in Ricdoon," Sandra shouted out. "As it's a nice evening we're going to turn the ponies out in a field. Then we're staying at a place called the Star Inn."

"It's not over yet." Sophie hugged Rocket, stuffing him with polos. "We get to do it all over again tomorrow and then it's the Bifton show and the musical ride."

"And you never know," said Kate with a wink. "At the end of all that we might find out we've won Riding School of the Year and then you'll all be famous." She kissed Archie's nose who clearly didn't understand a word and sighed with impatience.

The field was perfect, with post and rail fencing and short sweet grass just as ponies like it. They all rolled like mad as soon as we took off the tack, throwing up a load of dust which turned Archie and Buzby brown. We found out from the stables owner that one of the ponies in the group behind us had lost a shoe and had to retire. I shivered with horror. It would be awful if that happened to us.

"I feel as if I've ridden across the Sahara Desert bareback," Jodie groaned. She'd had to use her legs far more on Phantom than she ever did on Minstrel.

"I feel as if I've done the London Marathon." Emma let her legs go wobbly to show what she meant.

"I'm going to soak in the bath for three hours and use up all the hot water," Kate said.

"That'd be right." Steph screwed up her face. "Saint Kate to the rescue."

"What's happened to your mum?" Kate giggled. "She looks as if she's turned bow-legged."

It hadn't been as embarrassing as I'd thought having Mum on the trek and in some ways I was proud of her guts and her ability to learn to ride so quickly. But I nearly died when she presumed we'd be sharing the same bedroom and quickly dumped all my stuff in with the Six Pack and refused to come out. It was the first time I'd ever openly defied her.

We were the only group of trekkers at the Star Inn which made it less intimidating when we sat down for dinner. We all had chips, Cumbrian sausage, burgers and beans, followed by chocolate pudding, and nobody left a scrap. The staff were really nice and didn't talk down to us at all. Sandra announced that we had to draw names out of a hat because the manager had organized a special horsy murder mystery which was to be staged in the garden and sun lounge so that we wouldn't disturb the other guests.

Everybody went crazy with excitement. I was Mary King, Emma was Karen Dixon, and Sophie was Princess Anne. Steph was Pippa Funnell and ended up being the murder victim, poisoned and left to die in the summer house.

It turned out to be Max as Mark Todd who had done the dirty deed so that the path would be clear for him to win at Badminton and take over Pippa's horse. It was Sophie as Princess Anne who worked out how he did it and as she was part of our team we all won a prize. I was just thankful that I didn't have to act in public.

We dragged ourselves up the stair banister,

exhausted and stiff. Mum insisted on kissing me in front of everybody which made me feel about six. Jodie said if she could ever walk again it would be a miracle.

Emma peeled something off my back and handed it to me. "Looks like someone's sending you messages," she laughed without even reading it.

"What does it say?" Steph asked, leaning forward, but she was more interested in reliving the murder mystery for the hundredth time.

I screwed up the note and crammed it in my pocket. "Nothing," I said. "Let's get to bed."

The next morning, while the others went down to breakfast, I unscrewed the note and sat on the edge of the bed staring at it. It wasn't much of a message, just the word "Sickie" written in blue biro, but it still had the power to cut right through me.

Chapter Seven

The sun stopped shining at about lunchtime. Heavy grey cloud seemed to sit on top of the fells. It wasn't exactly cold but a mist started coming in from nowhere, swirling around the ponies' legs.

Rusty pricked his ears, listening to a far off sound, and Sandra reined in Doris and rechecked her map. "Another thirteen kilometres dropping down into a valley and we're there," she said. "First we've got to get up this ridge." We could see the hoof prints of the ride which had gone in front of us. A clear yellow arrow pointing straight on told us all we needed to know.

Rusty was really enjoying himself, ears pricked and striding out. Mum gasped as a waterfall came into view, cascading down the whole length of the hillside. It was magnificent. We all stared, stunned, lost in the beauty and wildness of the fells.

As we rode to the top of the ridge, leaning forward to take the weight off the ponies' backs, a chink of sunlight glinted through the greyness.

Near the waterfall, a rainbow, which had magically appeared, was illuminating the skyline.

"Isn't this beautiful," Mum breathed, lost in the moment.

Sophie, who was the arty one among us, went into raptures and talked about oils and painting and depths of colour.

By the time we'd got to the top of the ridge the sun was pouring through the clouds and the mist had lifted, as had everyone's spirits.

Emma got the giggles because Buzby had liquorice stuck to his front teeth and kept peeling back his top lip to show everyone.

We had a picnic and found a stream for the horses to drink from. Sandra looked more relaxed and in charge than yesterday. She said it was so fantastic she could happily become a professional trekker. Everyone was really enjoying themselves and didn't want the experience to end.

"Maybe we could do this every summer holidays," said Kate as she leaned back against a rock, rucking up her jodhpurs. "Brook House could organize its own riding holidays. We could go to Scotland, Wales, Cornwall . . ."

"Imagine riding on the beach," Jodie added, looking wistful.

"What about the moors? That would be something." Steph plaited Monty's forelock while he grazed happily.

"I want this holiday to go on and on for ever," Emma said, picking a wild flower and arranging it in Buzby's bridle.

"It needs to," Jodie said. "It'll take us a year to save up for the next one."

"Not like those two spoilt brats over there. Anything they want just gets handed to them on a plate," Kate whispered.

"Taggie's really nice," I insisted. "Honestly, you should give her a chance."

"Rachel, you get taken in by anybody. You're so pathetic."

"I am not!" I said hotly, standing up. "I'm not the baby you think I am."

"Half-time." Sophie stood up, resting a hand on my arm. "What were we just saying about all this being wonderful?"

Kate smirked, happy that she'd wound me up.

"It is," I muttered. "It's just the company."

"Rachel, what's got into you?" Steph looked really surprised.

Even though I knew Kate was often awful to me because she was unhappy with herself, I still found it difficult to forgive her sometimes. I tended to overreact to everything she said. I got up and deliberately went across to Taggie, leaving Rusty with Emma to graze.

"Oh, it's mummy's girl," Max grunted, stuffing his face with chocolate. I ignored him, determined to show that he hadn't upset me. And that he wouldn't in the future.

"Why don't you ride with me later?" Taggie smiled up at me.

"Thanks, that's a great idea." I felt a sense of smug satisfaction.

"Eh, I dare you to look down there," said Max, chuckling to himself as he pulled the wrapper off a Mars Bar. He pointed over the ridge.

I stepped away from him and peered over the edge. I saw the bleached bones of a sheep's carcass.

"Must have fallen," laughed Max. "Sheep are really thick."

I swallowed back a wave of nausea and stumbled away. A mass of cloud banked up again, blotting out the blue sky, and I shivered at the sudden change in temperature. The sunshine had all but gone.

"Rachel, I really think you could spend more time riding alongside me," Mum complained. "I did this for you, after all."

No you didn't, I thought bitterly. You did it so you could treat me like a baby, spoil my fun.

66

You're trying to live your life through mine. You're being overprotective and I hate it. I tightened my fingers on the reins and Rusty threw up his head, wondering what was going on.

"And I don't really want you talking to that Taggie," she said in a hushed voice. "I've heard all sorts of things about her."

"You said that about the Six Pack and now you think they're all right," I mumbled, keeping my eyes fixed between Rusty's ears.

"I'm only saying these things for your own good, Rachel. You should know that by now."

A silence followed. I stared down at the stony track wondering how many wild ponies had used it over the centuries. Rusty carefully picked his way forward, as sure-footed as a mountain goat.

"Don't you think you should put your jumper back on?" Mum glanced round at me. "It's getting damp, and you know your asthma always comes on if you get a cold."

"Mum, I'm fine."

"Well, you don't look it. In fact, you look perished. Take your hat off and pull your jumper over your head now, while I hold Rusty."

I knew Max was behind me, sniggering.

I did as she asked, poking my head through an arm and struggling like mad. Sandra dropped back on Doris and asked Mum if she'd mind helping with Sarah Jane who was only nine and feeling a bit homesick. Mum agreed immediately and I mouthed "thanks" to Sandra. By now I'd fallen back to near the rear of the ride.

"Feel better with your jumper on?" Max teased. "Don't want you getting a runny nose, do we?"

"Max, shut up." Taggie pushed her chestnut pony level with Rusty. "You can ride with your friends if you want," she said, smiling. "Don't let us cramp your style."

"No, no, it's all right." I could see Kate's red rucksack ahead and decided to stay where I was. The two thoroughbreds came up each side of me like police escorts.

"Well, the thing is," Taggie whispered, "we're just going to veer off to the right down that grassy track so we can have a canter. It's been a bit boring for the last hour or so. We'll only be gone ten minutes. Nobody will even miss us."

I sat upright suddenly, taken aback. A warning prickle crept up my spine, but I ignored it.

"I'll come with you," I blurted out, my voice sounding strange even to me. I wanted to get away from Mum. From the Six Pack. I didn't think about the consequences.

"When we get to that next bend of trees," Max whispered, "we'll break away. Nobody'll miss us for ages."

I felt my chest tighten with excitement. Rusty quickened his step, picking up my mood. Mum was chatting to Sandra, locked in conversation.

"OK, now!" cried Max, and he and Taggie wheeled their ponies off to the right, down a turfy path. Rusty followed, reluctantly leaving his friends. A branch whipped me in the face. "I bet you any money this will join back up with the main track and we'll be the ones waiting for them. Serves them right for being dozy," Max laughed.

And then they kicked their ponies on, hurtling forward in a flurry of hoofs. Rusty set off after them, bewildered at the sudden change of pace. I sat tight and kicked on, ignoring the spray of turf that scuffed back into my face. But I knew as soon as I set off that it was a mistake. I should have turned back then and there.

But I didn't. I kept going, trying to keep up even though it was impossible. Rusty didn't have the thoroughbreds' speed. We got further and further behind. And neither Max nor Taggie thought to look back. Taggie's laugh was the last I saw or heard of them. Suddenly, everything was deathly quiet. Just Rusty's footfalls and laboured breathing.

I started to panic. It hadn't been a straight track; there had been two or three forks. I hadn't had time to think, to memorize. I glanced round, scanning the horizon, but there was nothing that I could latch on to. Nothing remotely familiar. I shouted Taggie's name but my voice was whipped away on the circling air. How could she disappear like that? How could she leave me stranded?

Burning hot tears welled up. I swallowed them down because I had to keep my head. Surely the others would notice we were missing and come looking for us? Taggie and Max would probably come back to find me. It was only a matter of time before someone came. After all, they couldn't be that far away.

I snuffled back a sob and pushed Rusty forward, retracing my steps. I tried to ignore the black clouds looming closer and the patches of mist that seemed to be growing thicker. It just seemed worse because I was on my own.

"Hello, is there anyone there?" I cried.

A swarm of sheep rustled forward across the track and dipped down out of sight. Rusty snorted, splaying out his forefeet. It was getting darker. A mist seemed to be rising up out of the ground from nowhere. I couldn't believe this. How could it be happening? It was meant to be a dream holiday. Panic bubbled up inside me. Voices in my head told me I was a fool – that I deserved to be lost.

"Taggie! Max! Mum! Sandra!" I shouted till I was hoarse. One small mistake and I seemed to be going round in circles. Then we came to another fork. I couldn't see hoof prints one way or the other.

Droplets of moisture were clinging to my clothes now as the mist grew denser. The track dropped down abruptly. I couldn't see where I was going. Rusty started sliding... He couldn't keep his balance... The ground seemed to be giving way...

"Rusty!" My voice tore out of my chest. He crashed down onto his knees, dropping one shoulder. I flew over his neck, catapulting through the air and landing in what felt like prickly gorse. But no sooner had I winced with the pain than I was falling, rolling, tumbling. I snatched out at tussocks, stones, tree roots but I couldn't stop – I was out of control. Rusty neighed, bewildered, frightened, calling out.

I crashed against a rock, my back slamming into the cold hardness and bouncing the breath out of my body.

And then I lay still. Crumpled, bruised and shocked.

Rusty tried to get to me. "No, boy. No, go back!" Fear seared through me when I saw his shadowy outline trying to slide down the bank. He'd kill himself. "No, boy. Please, stay there." Even in the dim filtered light I could see the bank

71

was treacherous. But what now? Hot terror seized me. Rusty couldn't get down to me and I couldn't get up to him. It was too steep. I was trapped. Stuck in the bottom of a gully with no one knowing.

I screamed then. An instinctive reaction, but all it did was frighten Rusty and make him more determined to reach me. I had to think. I had to stay calm. The others couldn't be far away. But they'd never find me without help. I wasn't hurt but I could feel my chest tightening. I didn't have my inhaler. I had to control it by sheer will-power. Suddenly I made a decision.

"Go boy, find help!" Rusty edged closer, refusing to leave. I fell back, gasping for breath. It was getting dark. I couldn't spend a night on the fells – I couldn't. "Rusty, you've got to find the others," I whispered. Suddenly he seemed to understand . . .

Chapter Eight

I lay back against the rock, listening to the total silence. Had Rusty gone to fetch help? Had he really understood?

The last I'd heard of him was his hoofs clattering back up out of the dip. What if he hurt himself? What if I'd done the wrong thing sending him away?

I closed my eyes and felt the fat tears rolling down my cheeks. What had possessed me to listen to Taggie and do something so stupid? Everybody knew that people got lost on the fells – it was on the news often enough. That's why it was a properly organized ride, with adults, and arrows marking the way.

I'd followed Taggie because I'd wanted to impress her. How stupid could you get? Now I was paying the price. I was bruised and sore, but at least that was all. I rubbed my hands together, thankful that I was wearing my jumper. What if they didn't find me? What if I had to stay here all night? My thoughts turned to wolves and wild cats, escaped from zoos and living wild. I could die out here. People did. A slow, painful, torturous death.

A ripple of terror shot through me. Immediately I felt as if my windpipe was being crushed. My chest tightened as if a metal band had been fixed round it. I had to stay calm, think positive. I dragged in a ragged breath and then exhaled deeply. One, two, one, two. Calmly does it.

The minutes trickled into hours. Where was everyone? Not a single sound; not even a sheep, a deer or a bird. It was unnatural. I tried three times to scrabble up the bank but did no more than scratch at the soil, slipping backwards every time. I just ended up feeling dizzy and frantic.

I was going to die. That's all there was to it. They'd find my bleached bones like those of that sheep. I told myself to get a grip and to stop being so melodramatic. I almost pinched myself. Everybody would be out looking. I pulled my knees up to my chin and tried to shrug off the damp.

"Just let Rusty be all right," I whispered. "Don't let him have got lost too."

"Rachel!" Mum's voice cut through the mist. I was on my feet in seconds. More voices – Sandra's, Emma's.

"I'm here!" I yelled, screeching so loud I thought my lungs would burst. I lunged at the bank again, trying to make a noise, bashing my hands against grass sods. "I'm here, down here!" I picked up a dead branch and started thrashing it against a wizened tree. Then I heard Rusty's familiar deep whicker and saw movement. Coats, heads, people. Friends. My friends. "Mum!"

Relief sent silent tears pouring down my cheeks.

"Are you all right?" Mum's frightened face appeared over the bank. She was scrabbling on her hands and knees, her voice hollow with panic.

"Don't come down! It's too steep." I shielded my eyes with a hand, trying to focus in the drizzly mist. "I'm fine, Mum. I'm OK."

"Someone's going to have to fetch help," Sandra shouted. "We'll need ropes. Are you sure you're all right? Nothing broken?"

"No, honestly. Just a bit shaken up. How's Rusty?" My voice tightened.

"He deserves a medal." Emma was hyper with excitement. "He led us to you, Rachel. Can you believe it? If it wasn't for him you could have been here all night."

"He's going to be a star," Steph's voice rung out. "The next Black Beauty. The life-saving pony."

"We'll go for help." Taggie's voice made me jerk back as if stung. So they'd found their way back. Lucky them.

"Don't even think about it. Haven't you done

75

enough harm already?" Mum's voice was savage. It was like listening to a drama on the radio, imagining the characters' faces. For a bizarre moment I started giggling and then I sagged completely and started sobbing.

"Rachel!"

"I'll go," Sandra said. "I can't risk someone else getting lost. It's ten kilometres to the finish line. I'll bring back help. Taggie, I'll ride your pony. Nobody move until I get back. Hold on, Rachel, I won't be long."

I imagined her putting her foot in the stirrup and gathering up the reins. Then I heard the thrum of hoof beats.

Emma spent the next hour telling me bad jokes. Mum seemed to calm down once she realized I truly wasn't hurt. It was good to hear my friends' voices. Nobody mentioned how stupid I'd been. Nobody mentioned the cold and the damp.

I heard the quad bike first. The relief was like an anaesthetic. I wanted to curl up and sleep.

Within no time at all there was a flurry of activity and a man lowering himself on a rope, grinning at me through a bristly beard.

"Got yourself in a spot of bother, eh?"

"You could say that."

He showed me how to hold on to the rope while his partner winched me up.

"You're a lucky lass not to have hurt yourself. All the same I think your mum'll want you to be checked over at the hospital."

My fingers throbbed with the sudden friction from the rope. Each painful centimetre brought me closer to the top. Then it dawned on me that I must look a mess. There was a rip in my jumper and mud down my left side. I could sense everybody holding their breath at the top.

"Rachel!" Mum threw herself forward, arms open. "Thank God you're all right."

"Oh Mum." I wrapped my arms around her and felt the warmth flood back in. "I'm sorry."

"We'll lead the two ponies and then you and your mum can ride on the back of the quads," said Sandra.

"Rusty!" I scoured round urgently for him.

Sophie led him forward. I pushed my fingers into his furry neck and kissed his nose. Then he started licking my face and nuzzling my hair.

"You ought to have seen him, Rachel. He kept trotting round refusing to be caught until we followed him. He led us straight here."

"Clever, clever boy," I murmured, wondering how I'd ever be able to thank him. When I looked up I caught Taggie's guilty eyes and looked swiftly away.

The two men ushered me onto the pillion seat

of the first quad and wrapped a blanket round my legs. It was only then that I realized I was shaking all over. The drive back over the fells was bumpy and exhausting. We came really close to Lake Windermere but I hadn't got the energy to look up and focus through the veil of mist.

A car was waiting when we reached the finishing post. The hospital was fifteen kilometres away and Mum sat in the back seat, holding my hand all the way. I'd never seen her look so stripped of energy, so ragged with worry. A doctor examined me, looking in my eyes and listening to my chest, asking me questions and mumbling about horse riding being dangerous and no place for heroics.

All I wanted to do was go to sleep.

One of the trek's organizers gave us a lift to the Ship Inn where we were staying the night. All the ponies were being stabled at a local riding school. Bifton showground was only five kilometres away.

It was a large guest house, full of trekkers running high on adrenalin after the ride and in anticipation of the next day. It all felt so distant — as if I was an observer looking down at myself from afar. A group of adult riders were comparing the virtues of Connemaras to those of New Forests. Everywhere people were making plans and running through the musical ride for the show.

That should have been me. Instead, Mum led me up the stairs and tucked me up in bed with strict orders to rest while she went and found some soup and hot chocolate.

The door burst open and the Six Pack tumbled in, checking that Mum was well out of sight down the corridor. Emma was grinning and Steph was clutching a pile of chocolate bars and magazines which she poured into my lap. Kate thumped a bottle of Coca-Cola onto the bedside table and peered at me as if she was a doctor.

"It's not fair," Emma moaned, picking white hairs off her bright purple jumper. "How come you get to have all the fun?"

They weren't holding it against me – even though it was a Six Pack rule that we did everything together and put things to the vote.

"We're just glad you're all right," Jodie said, reading my thoughts.

"You ought to see the stables the ponies are in," Sophie said. "It's an American-style barn with automatic waterers and rubber-matting floors."

"Never," I said, slipping into the old chit-chat as if I'd never been trapped down a gully and lost in one of the wildest parts of England.

"Buzby's really jealous because Rusty's the star," Sophie went on. "He deliberately stood on Emma's foot and dug up his bed."

79

"My legs are aching like mad," Steph moaned, and then caught sight of my black and blue arms and burst out laughing. "Sorry, Rachel, I guess you need the hot bath more than me. Did you really send Rusty back to fetch help? I mean, did he understand you?"

The room seemed fuzzy and my eyelids kept dragging shut but nobody seemed to notice. Emma decided to bounce on the bed to see if my mattress was as good as hers and Kate wound everyone up by saying the only food they served at the Ship Inn was Cumbrian black pudding.

Mum walked in the door just as Emma shrieked and sent a pillow flying across to Steph.

"I think Rachel needs peace and quiet," Mum said in a strained voice. "If you'd all kindly leave now." She walked across to the bedside table carrying a tray, and put it down carefully. Then she sat on the edge of the bed and felt my head.

"Rusty's fine," I said. "Isn't that good news – for tomorrow, I mean?"

Mum paled instantly. "Rachel, you're not suggesting for one minute that you're going to ride?"

"Why not?

"Why not? You nearly killed yourself today. It was all my fault. I should have been watching you closer – I should have seen it coming. I shouldn't even be letting you ride. What kind of a mother am I?"

"Mum, stop it, I'm all right. Can't you see that you just make things a million times worse?"

She looked stunned, as if I'd slapped her across the face. I plucked at the bedspread awkwardly, struggling to find the words to explain myself better.

"After all I've done for you, how can you say that?" Her bottom lip wobbled and she frantically smoothed the creases out of her skirt. "If your dad could hear you now."

"Mum, you've been fantastic, brilliant, but I'm not a baby any more. I don't need taking out of school. I don't need to miss sports or stay in when the pollen count is high. I don't need to be wrapped up in cotton wool. I want to lead a normal life, Mum."

"And you think I'm stopping you? Well that's thanks and gratitude, isn't it? If you're so grown-up all of a sudden, why did you sneak off today? It was one of the most stupid things you've ever done."

"Yes, and I've learnt my lesson. Mum, I've learnt not to be intimidated by other people's ignorance and rudeness. I've learnt the hard way, but I've got there. Honestly."

The silence stretched out for an eternity.

81

"Mum, I want to ride tomorrow. The doctor said I could, but I want to do it with your blessing."

She pursed her lips, smoothing her skirt. Then she drew in a long breath and took my hand in hers. I knew she'd listened. I knew she was trying to let go. "Right then. I'd better go and iron your jodhpurs."

Chapter Nine

I'd never been to a major agricultural show. Kate spent the whole of breakfast explaining how there would be cattle, sheep, goats, pigs, as well as showjumping, show-pony classes, parachute jumpers, daredevil bike riders, and the whole of the Household Cavalry. Of course I knew all this already but Kate liked to spout her knowledge.

"Princess Anne!" cried Steph, bursting through the door.

"What?"

"Princess Anne is going to be there for the native pony pilgrimage." Steph spoke slowly and clearly as if we were all stupid. Sophie shot under the tablecloth, supposedly to salvage a sausage but more likely to compose herself. Sophie hated the limelight more than anybody and meeting a member of the royal family was bound to paralyse her with terror.

"I hope you girls are going to scrub your fingernails," Mum commented, suddenly animated at the thought of royalty. She was clutching a tube of toothpaste which Emma had requested, and started squeezing it unconsciously with excitement.

Since our conversation last night, Mum had been one hundred and ten per cent supportive. She'd taken it upon herself to see that we all looked immaculate and professionally turned out. Earlier, at the overnight stables, she'd even taken a box of soap powder and started scrubbing at Buzby's yellow stable stains which we were all convinced he'd got deliberately. Buzby was so taken aback by the ferocity of her cleaning that he stood as good as gold and for once didn't pull a single stunt, not even tipping up his bucket of water or standing on the hosepipe.

We'd left the riding school and returned to the Ship Inn to get washed and changed, or fed, watered and groomed as Sandra put it. Everyone in our group was buzzing with anticipation. It was really happening. We were going to the Bifton show.

"There's going to be someone from *Emmerdale* and someone from *EastEnders* there," said Jodie who was reading last night's evening paper. Mum shot up and headed for the door, saying she must redo her hair. She had a secret crush on one of the characters. Max bumped into her, then meekly stepped to one side and slithered into her chair with a plateful of food. The atmosphere chilled to arctic temperatures.

"Can you smell something rotten?" Emma held her nose.

"Shut up," Jodie hissed. "There's no need to go down to his level."

Max and Taggie were leaving that morning. Mr and Mrs Carrington had come up with a horse trailer and Steph had heard them shouting at Max in the office.

He wolfed down his breakfast, totally ignoring us. When he stood up, he dodged past me and whispered "Sickie" in my ear. I didn't flinch. I didn't respond at all.

But as he scuttled for the door the last laugh was on him. His trousers were covered in white toothpaste which Mum had left on the seat. He blushed scarlet as the Six Pack fell about laughing.

"They always say those who dish it out can't take it back," Steph shrieked. The door slammed shut, shuddering on its hinges.

"I wanted to say sorry," Taggie mumbled. We were standing in the foyer of the guest house. Taggie's rucksack was propped near her feet and Max's parents hovered nearby, reading leaflets on the Lakes.

"I'm sorry we made you feel bad. If it's any

85

consolation, Max is being grounded for eternity, and I probably will be too when I get home."

"Thanks." From now on I wouldn't be influenced by people's ignorance.

"Mum's enrolling me to help out in a swimming class for asthmatics," she went on. "I think I'll drag Max along too. It'll do him good."

"Yes," I said. "Well, bye then." And I walked back into the dining room, back to my real friends, feeling a zillion times more grown up.

"Everyone's fine at Brook House and Guy is all set to catch the train to London for tonight's ceremony." Sandra was leaning over the table, animatedly filling everyone in on her phone call.

"If *only* we could win . . ." Steph mused, no doubt dreaming of personal fame.

"We won't know that until tonight," Sandra said. "Guy promised to ring straight after the presentation."

"We will," said Emma, busily wrapping up sausages in tissue for the dog at the stables. "It's written in the stars."

"I don't want to give everyone indigestion but don't you think we should get moving?" Jodie looked tense. She was always half an hour early for everything, including the dentist.

"The great moment has arrived," Kate said

sombrely, and, shuddering with anticipation, we all dived for the door.

There were ponies everywhere. Native breeds in all shapes and sizes filing into the showground in endless streams. Policemen littered the road giving instructions. There seemed to be far more pony pilgrimage people than had been accounted for. The Brook House riders and ponies entered the showground through the main entrance, directly behind a group of Highlands.

"Never mind fifty riders, there's hundreds," Sandra squeaked, terrified of losing one of us in the chaos. From tiny children on Shetland ponies to pensioners on Dales and Highlands, every breed was represented and every age group.

Buzby stared fixedly at a Welsh lookalike, holding up scores of riders. Emma's legs and arms rotated like windmills in an effort to get him moving. Kate was at a loss when Archie charged after a band of New Forest mares, strutting like a peacock to get their attention.

"All stay together," Sandra shrieked, to no avail. Rusty plodded on between Rocket and Phantom, totally unperturbed. Even when a hot-air balloon swooped nerve-rackingly low, tilting its basket and sending half the showjumpers and show horses into a swirl of rearing and bucking.

"This is why we're celebrating native ponies," Emma preened. "Because they're so level-headed, so sensible."

Buzby then decided that he coudn't wait any longer for a meal, dragged the reins deftly out of her hands and started tearing at the sweet lush grass. Archie did the same. A trail of ponies spanning three pathways had to wait until they'd finished.

Harassed stewards ushered us into a roped collecting ring where we'd be called for the musical ride. It was getting as squashed as sardines in a tin.

"I can't breathe," said Jodie, looking claustrophobic.

"It should be me who's saying that," I laughed.

Emma and Steph appeared on foot holding ice-cream cones. They bit off the bottom and sucked out the strawberry ripple.

"Who got you those?" Kate was fuming as she held on to Buzby and Monty.

"Mrs W."

"Who's Mrs W?"

"Rachel's mum." Emma rolled her eyes as if Kate was thick.

Mum appeared in the midst of a horde of people carrying more ice-cream cones, and for a moment I swelled with pride. I was glad she was here. Glad she'd taken up riding. She wasn't just any mum. She was special.

"Here, grab these." She pulled out a sheaf of papers from under her arm. "Far too many people have turned up, so they're picking fifty people for the display and then the rest are coming in for the finale in rows of ten. These are instructions for the routine. Look as if you know it by heart and you're bound to get picked."

She glanced round surreptitiously. "Most of these don't look as if they know a serpentine from a figure-of-eight." Neither did Mum until five minutes ago.

A lot of the ponies looked half asleep, as did their riders. Apparently, some people had trekked a hundred and fifty kilometres. Sandra rushed across from a blue and white tent to say that they were running behind with the motorbike daredevils who were having problems with one of their props, and that the mayor had dragged Princess Anne off to look at some Lincoln Reds.

Sophie had gone grey with nerves. I felt as if my stomach was practising for the high jump. Emma had somehow borrowed a pair of binoculars and was regaling us with details of the people in the members' tent and what they were doing.

"Waiting for us to make fools of ourselves," said Jodie, nervously picking at her rubber reins. Red,

89

white and blue smoke puffed out from behind the motorbikes, and they roared out of the ring to a round of applause.

Suddenly, a steward in a yellow bib with a red face was barking at us to take our places. "You are in the musical display, aren't you?"

We bustled forward to join a queue behind the Millhouse Equestrian Centre.

"I want to be sick," moaned Sophie. Amazingly, I was fizzing with the undercurrent of tension. Any second now we'd be cantering into the huge arena. I felt the warmth of Rusty's neck and knew he'd do anything I wanted.

The national anthem struck up, wafting through the powerful loudspeakers, so different from those at local shows. I nearly died when I looked up at a shadow in the sky and saw a massive crane with a TV man hanging out filming us. We were going to be on telly!

A steward pulled back the rope and we cantered onto the perfectly preserved turf where the likes of John Whittaker had wowed crowds. It was our turn now.

I caught snatches of the commentator's speech, saw the crowds of people, ten deep, listening attentively, watching us. "Ladies and gentlemen. Our heritage. The nine native breeds of the British Isles brought together for you today in a pony pilgrimage which has raised thousands for charity and heightened the awareness and appreciation of our national treasure."

A line of tiny Shetlands blasted across the arena at a flat-out gallop, followed by the Highlands and the New Forests.

"It's their hardiness, stamina, sure-footedness and much more which has made them special for so many generations . . ."

My heart flipped over as a woman pulled me back to join the Dartmoors. Kate and Emma went forward to join the Welsh. I was burning up with adrenalin.

"Wait . . . wait . . . Now!" The Dartmoors charged forward, Rusty locked in the middle, enjoying every second. He was pulling my arms out!

We circled at the bottom as the Connemaras hurtled towards us, looking as if they were unable to stop. Jodie was grinning her head off. The audience were clapping louder than ever, thoroughly enjoying the specatacle. It was a roaring success. The anthem belted out louder and we all took our places, circling the main arena, preparing to turn in on the right beat – all together.

"What a cavalcade!" The commentator was getting more and more excited. Everyone thundered across the arena and turned in the right direction. Tiny Shetlands were scurrying next to bigger Highlands and New Forests. It was a fantastic sight. I was bursting with pride.

I had to concentrate – couldn't make a mistake. We were coming across the diagonal now and the ride split into two groups going in opposite directions. Emma passed me. She was grinning and her hat had slipped down over her eyes. The audience were clapping in time to the anthem. The atmosphere was electric.

It all passed so fast. I could go on and on. I knew the ride like the back of my hand. Some of the ponies had got completely overexcited and bucked off their riders, but nobody was hurt and it all added to the entertainment. It was over too soon and we had to file back out into the collecting ring.

"Would Rachel Whitehead on Rusty from Brook House Riding School come back to the centre of the arena for a presentation . . ." the commentator's voice rang out.

My blood froze. Could it really be me? "Ladies and gentlemen, I want you to give a big hand to a very brave pony who saved his rider's life less than twenty-four hours ago . . ." It was me!

The clapping was deafening as dear, sweet Rusty left the others and cantered back, ears pricked, towards a group of people . . . and Princess Anne!

Chapter Ten

"What did she say?" The Six Pack clustered round, bursting with excitement.

Rusty trotted into the collecting ring complete with a gold sash, a striped green rug, and a red, white and blue rosette. I was still on cloud nine, unable to take it in. I'd shaken hands with Princess Anne! We'd done a lap of honour and the crowds had gone wild, clapping louder than ever. It was unbelievable. Miraculous. Rusty was famous.

"Rachel, what did she say?" Jodie caught the sleeve of my riding jacket.

"That Rusty was a very special pony and she'd always had a soft spot for Dartmoors, and that I was very lucky to ride him."

"You jammy devil," said Kate, nearly dying of envy.

"And she admired my badge," I added, touching the special Six Pack badge which had been given to us by the mega-famous horse therapist, Josh le Fleur.

"Cool." Steph was elated. "We're now known in royal circles."

Mum pushed past the crowd, elbowing them out of the way, tears glistening in her eyes. There was no need for words. We hugged each other and then Rusty.

"I think we'd better move out of the way before there's a stampede," Jodie said, ever practical. Native ponies were everywhere.

Someone in a BBC sweatshirt with a cameraman behind him was approaching at speed. "Rachel Whitehead?"

Just as I was about to answer, Sophie's dad sprang out of the crowds, diving past a Welsh cob, brandishing what looked like a letter.

He was worn to a frazzle. In fact, I'd never seen him so dishevelled. "Thank goodness I've found you." He rested an arm on Rusty's rump while he got his breath back. "There's been a terrible mix-up."

My blood drained cold. For a moment I wondered if Rusty would have to give back his beautiful rug and rosette.

"I'm really sorry, girls." He looked distraught. "I don't know how it got lost."

"Dad, you're not making any sense," said Sophie, pushing Rocket forward.

"Guy's been frantically trying to get hold of me.

You see, there's a new award for the most out-standing group of riding school pupils . . . And you've been nominated."

"Dad!"

"I know, I know, but the letter got lost under a pile of accounts. I've been so busy, I . . ." He rubbed at his unshaven face with both hands. "The presentation starts in just under an hour. In London."

"But Dad, we're in Cumbria."

"I know. I'm so sorry, girls. I tried to tell you as soon as possible."

"Excuse me, am I right in understanding that these girls have won an award?" The man in the TV sweatshirt pushed forward.

"Nominated," corrected Mum, shooting him a smile. "It's a chance in a lifetime." She was enthralled.

The TV man ran his tongue over his dry lips and looked at Dad. "The thing is, I might just be able to help."

"Wait till I tell Belinda at school about this. She won't believe it." Emma stuck her face up to the window, totally unperturbed.

Kate and Sophie looked petrified and did nothing but finger their seatbelts as if they had half a mind to jump out. We were all numb with shock.

As if we'd accidentally stepped into someone else's life and any minute we'd wake up and be cleaning tack back at Brook House.

The helicopter's propellers whipped round furiously at a million miles an hour. Finally, we landed. The top international showjumper who'd hired the helicopter got out to shake our hands and wish us well. It was like a dream. He was about to fly over the Channel to compete in a big Grand Prix in France.

"It's another world," Steph breathed, still trembling from the experience. Our words got snatched away in the wind, and then we were climbing into a taxi and streaking along to Grosvenor House. I don't know what was more scary, the helicopter or slicing through traffic on the London roads. I had to grip my stomach as we flew over a bump and whizzed past Buckingham Palace.

"I can't believe this is happening." Jodie stared out of the window at the chaos of people and traffic.

"Guy's going to wait on the doorstep," Kate said, biting her nails.

We knew this already but it was Kate's way of sounding important.

"We're here!" Steph shrieked.

Kate paid the taxi driver, dropping the change

on the pavement and making it quite obvious that we hadn't got a clue what we were doing.

"Are you sure you know where you're going?" The taxi driver leaned over, concerned. By now he knew everything about us minus our birth dates and favourite colours.

"You made it!" Guy was at our side in seconds, reassuring the taxi driver and us for that matter. We hardly recognized him in his posh dinner suit and bow tie. His hair was slicked back with gel and there wasn't a trace of horse anywhere.

"You look like a movie star," Emma gushed.

"Come on, they've started the awards." And as he stuffed tickets into our hands and we ran up the steps to the swing doors I knew this was going to be one of the special moments of our lives.

"Wow!" Steph turned pink. Inside a huge room, seated at round tables, were hundreds of guests, all immaculate in smart dresses and suits.

"The nominees are at the front," Guy whispered, and we curdled with embarrassment as we slithered forward, trying not to be noticed in our jodhpurs, boots and jackets. Two hundred pairs of beady curious eyes fixed on us as we scraped back seats and tried to blend into the scenery.

There were two people on stage reading out names and I instantly recognized the woman as Joanna Smiley, Editor of *In the Saddle*. We'd met her when the magazine asked Brook House to feature in a photo story. The other person was a man and Guy whispered that he was the Managing Director. All round the room were huge posters of famous riders reading the weekly magazine. It was only then that I noticed a few famous people in the audience, and quickly focused on my napkin.

The presenters moved on to the award for the most outstanding riding instructor and I saw Guy's jaw tense with disappointment. He hadn't been nominated but we could all vouch that he was a brilliant instructor and totally dedicated. The person who won looked really nice and had helped teach hundreds of underprivileged children in London to learn to ride.

Suddenly whistles went up from all corners of the room and the other nominees in our age group started standing up and turning round to gawp, hardly able to contain themselves.

"The award for the most popular up-and-coming showjumper . . ."

The magazine readers themselves had voted for this and everyone was craning to see if the nominees were in the room. I relaxed back into my chair and started to really enjoy myself. We had a fantastic view of the stage and, as Emma said, we could almost see up the winners' noses, we were so close.

A screech went up as the presenter announced the winner's name and Guy Goosen marched down the main aisle, hardly recognizable without his jodhpurs and famous horse, Sagrat, but looking incredibly gorgeous. Kate, Sophie and Steph swooned hopelessly, but Emma was saving herself for Carl Hester who she was convinced was here and who she'd voted for six times, breaking the rules.

It was ages before the room was quiet enough for Guy Goosen to make his speech. We practically had to put Emma in a straitjacket when Carl Hester won the award for the most popular dressage rider and arrived on stage.

"Teenage hormones," Guy tutted, looking bemused. Emma was screaming and crying with joy at the same time. She nearly fainted when Carl winked at her and threw a glove into the audience which, miraculously, she managed to catch, almost giving herself a hernia in the process.

Mary King won the award for eventing which I was really pleased about because I thought she was such a nice person and a wonderful horsewoman.

"Moving on now to the award which you've all been waiting for – Riding School of the Year."

We all sat bolt upright, clutching each other's hands. Jodie strained every nerve, waiting and listening. This is what she'd wanted Brook House to achieve ever since she'd first arrived at the riding school and it had been a shambles with no direction. Guy tensed as well. It was so important to the school to win recognition. The amount of lessons would double overnight. We had a good chance, I knew that. We could win. We had to win.

Joanna Smiley read down the list of nominees painstakingly slowly. After each announcement there was a loud cheer which filled the room. When it came to Brook House we screamed ourselves hoarse.

Then silence as Joanna composed herself for the announcement.

"And the winner is . . ." we all pressed one hand on our Six Pack badges, waiting and willing for the right words, "Parkside Equestrian Centre."

The disappointment was crucifying. We felt numb and despairing, and refused to accept it. How could they not choose Brook House? Jodie rested her elbows on the table, pressing a hand on each side of the bridge of her nose. I knew she was crying. The rest of us couldn't speak. It was like the bottom had been knocked out of our world. We'd all been so convinced we'd win.

"Clap! Clap!" Guy urged, hissing through his teeth. We mustn't be bad losers.

We had to congratulate the winners. I clapped

and smiled until my jaw felt as if it would crack. The rest of the Six Pack did the same.

When it came to the speech we found out that Parkside had specialized in riding for the disabled and had done a huge amount nationally to raise money and promote the cause. After hearing that we weren't quite so disappointed. We could see why they had won. We gave them a genuinely enthusiastic clap when they left the stage.

There were another couple of awards but we were too heavy-hearted to take any notice. It felt as if someone had dumped a load of bricks on our table. The atmosphere was that heavy.

"Moving on to the final award which we've only introduced this year and which we feel will be a huge success in motivating young people in the future . . ." Joanna Smiley paused, waiting for everyone's attention, "Riding School Pupils of the Year."

We all looked up, alert, but slumped again. There was no chance of us winning. We had to just be grateful and honoured that we'd been nominated. And it was an honour, after all.

"There's always next year," Guy whispered, recovering from the blinding disappointment.

I tuned into Joanna Smiley's words again as she read out the nominees.

"We have decided to give the award this year to

a group of pupils who we believe have gone above and beyond the call of duty in supporting their riding school. They've shown a passionate interest, not just in the activities of the riding school but in the ponies and people who are involved. We want to acknowledge their dedication and initiative."

Emma was running a biro up and down her forefinger and thumb. Jodie and Steph were dazed and switched off.

It was a few moments before we recognized the words "Brook House Six Pack".

Emma shot back in her chair, nearly keeling over. There was an expectant silence as the audience waited for someone to stand up.

Joanna spoke into the microphone. "Would Jodie, Kate, Sophie, Rachel, Emma and Steph make their way up to the stage."

Guy had to practically push us out of our seats. My legs were like jelly. We jostled together for support. Steph tripped up the three steps. I kept having to tell myself it wasn't a dream! Joanna arranged us around her so that nobody was hidden. I didn't know what to do with my hands. Emma looked out directly at the audience and then blushed crimson, dropping her eyes to the floor.

"Congratulations, girls, your names are going to be the very first to be engraved on the trophy." She must have felt like she was talking to a group of zombies. Jodie clutched the trophy awkwardly as if it would break if she squeezed too tightly. Steph and Kate stared at it as if it was an albatross or something. I was just too shocked to do anything.

Joanna smiled warmly and addressed the audience. "Ladies and gentlemen, I'd like you to put your hands together for a group of very special girls. Not only have they succeeded in keeping Brook House Riding School open against all odds, and, on a couple of occasions, tracking down criminal influences, but they have all dealt with personal difficulties and shown tireless devotion to the ponies and horses. They have been at the forefront of fund-raising campaigns and are true young ambassadors for riding at grass-roots level. I hope the Six Pack will be an inspiration to all other pony-mad young people in the country."

There was a huge cheer and Jodie stumbled towards the microphone to make a speech. We hadn't prepared anything. Jodie thanked our parents, Guy, Sandra, Sophie's dad for coming to the rescue, Mrs Brentford who still had a part-share in the school, and most of all the horses and ponies who made Brook House the incredibly special place that it was. She thanked *In the Saddle* for voting for us and then she thanked each of us for being her friends and for always being there when she needed us. By now we were all crying and hugging each other. That was what the Six Pack was for – being there for each other and for our four-legged friends.

The six of us took it in turns to hold the trophy aloft, and grinned as Guy stood up, clapping his hands above his head, and a photographer zoomed in for some close-up pictures. It was the best moment of my life and we'd proved that ordinary girls could achieve great things with riding school ponies. We couldn't wish for anything else.

"Thank you," we all whispered.

"Thanks, Rusty," I mouthed.

At last our dream had come true.

And so could yours!